I Knew
You Would,
I Knew
You Could

Hannah Manning

ISBN 978-1-0980-2961-6 (paperback)
ISBN 978-1-0980-2962-3 (digital)

Christian Faith Publishing, Inc.
832 Park Avenue
Meadville, PA 16335
www.christianfaithpublishing.com

Printed in the United States of America

Dedicated to my beautiful children.

Phil. 4:13 "I can do all things through Christ who gives me strength."

I knew you would, I knew you could

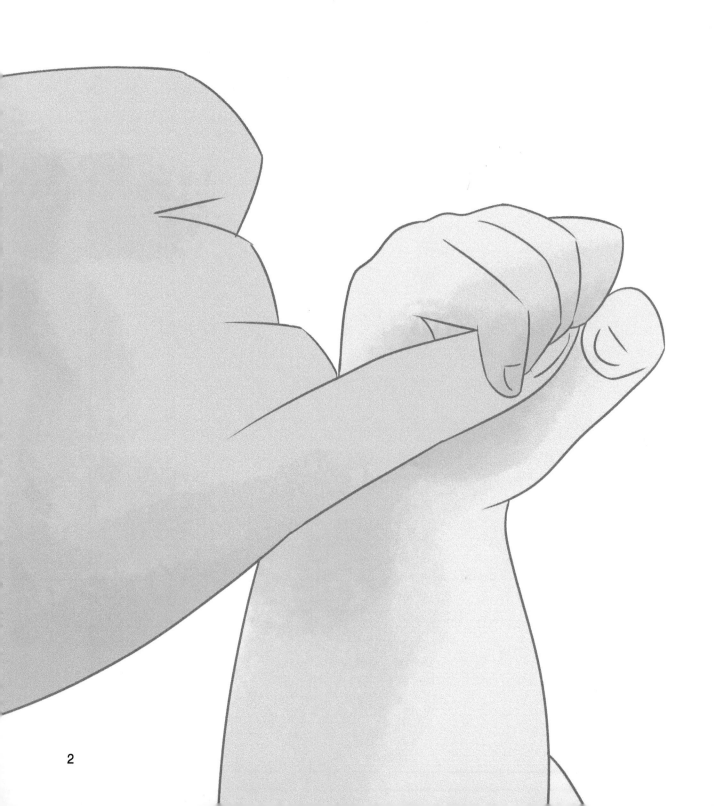

You'd grab and hold

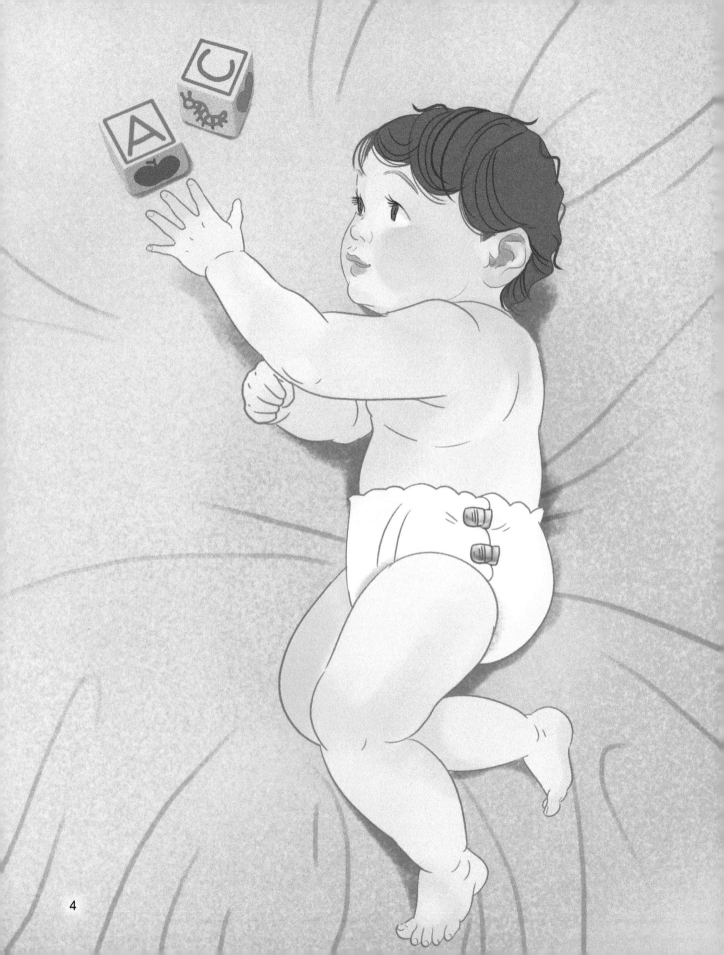

You'd lie and roll

You'd bounce and jump
You'd bonk and bump

You'd sit and crawl
But that's not all…

You'd stand and walk
You'd stumble and fall

You'd squeal and squawk
You'd mumble and talk

You'd smile and play
You'd clap and wave

You'd meet the challenge of each new day

You'd learn to eat, to chew, to drink
You'd learn to move, to stop, to think

13

You'd learn to dress,
to tie your shoes

You'd learn to comb your hair
and brush your teeth too

You'd learn to do what big kids do

You'd learn to write and read

Say your ABCs

Sing and paint, color, create

You'd learn to share and be kind
To matter, to mind

To give when it's hard, to run the race far
To never give up and always look up

Sometimes it takes a little work

Sometimes it takes a lot

But one thing's for sure,

One thing's for certain

You gave it all you got

I knew you would, I knew you could

About the Author

Hannah Manning is a mom of three in the beautiful state of Maine. Her children inspired this book, with all the milestones that come with age and the growing process. As a parent, she knows that every child grows at their own pace, but there never is a doubt that they will attain it. She hopes that this will be an encouragement to all children in the season that they're in that anything is possible!

CPSIA information can be obtained
at www.ICGtesting.com
Printed in the USA
BVHW021630260421
605873BV00016B/2015